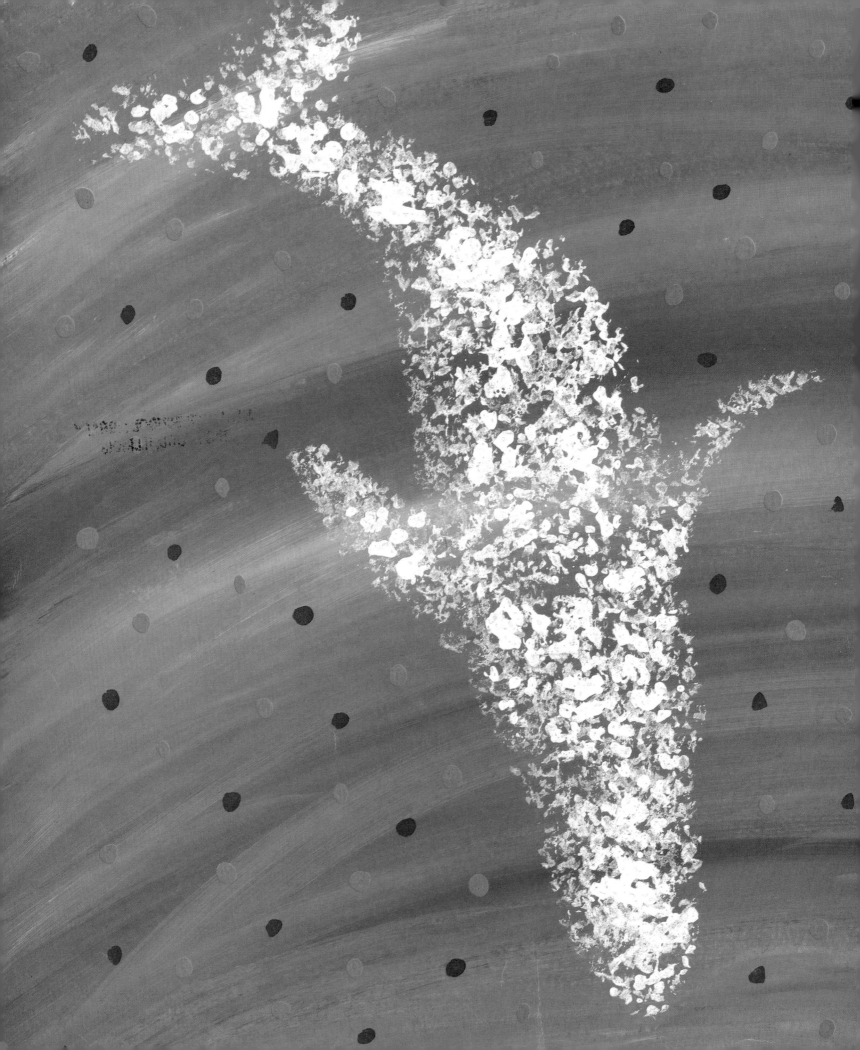

THE WHALES

WRITTEN AND ILLUSTRATED BY

Cynthia Rylant

THE BLUE SKY PRESS

An Imprint of Scholastic Inc. · New York

THE BLUE SKY PRESS

Copyright © 1996 by Cynthia Rylant

All rights reserved.

No part of this publication may be reproduced or stored
in a retrieval system or transmitted in any form or by any
means, electronic, mechanical, photocopying, recording, or
otherwise, without written permission of the publisher.

For information regarding permission, please write to:
Permissions Department,
The Blue Sky Press, an imprint of Scholastic Inc.,
555 Broadway, New York, New York 10012.

The Blue Sky Press is a trademark of Scholastic Inc.

Library of Congress Cataloging-in-Publication Data
Rylant, Cynthia.
The Whales / by Cynthia Rylant.
p.   cm.
Summary: Poetically describes the wonder of whales—
what they look like, how they behave, and where they live.
ISBN 0-590-58285-2
[1. Whales—Fiction.]   I. Title.
PZ7.R982Wh   1996   [E]—dc20   95-15298   CIP   AC

12 11 10 9 8 7 6 5 4 3 2 1   6 7 8 9/9 0/0   46

First printing, April 1996

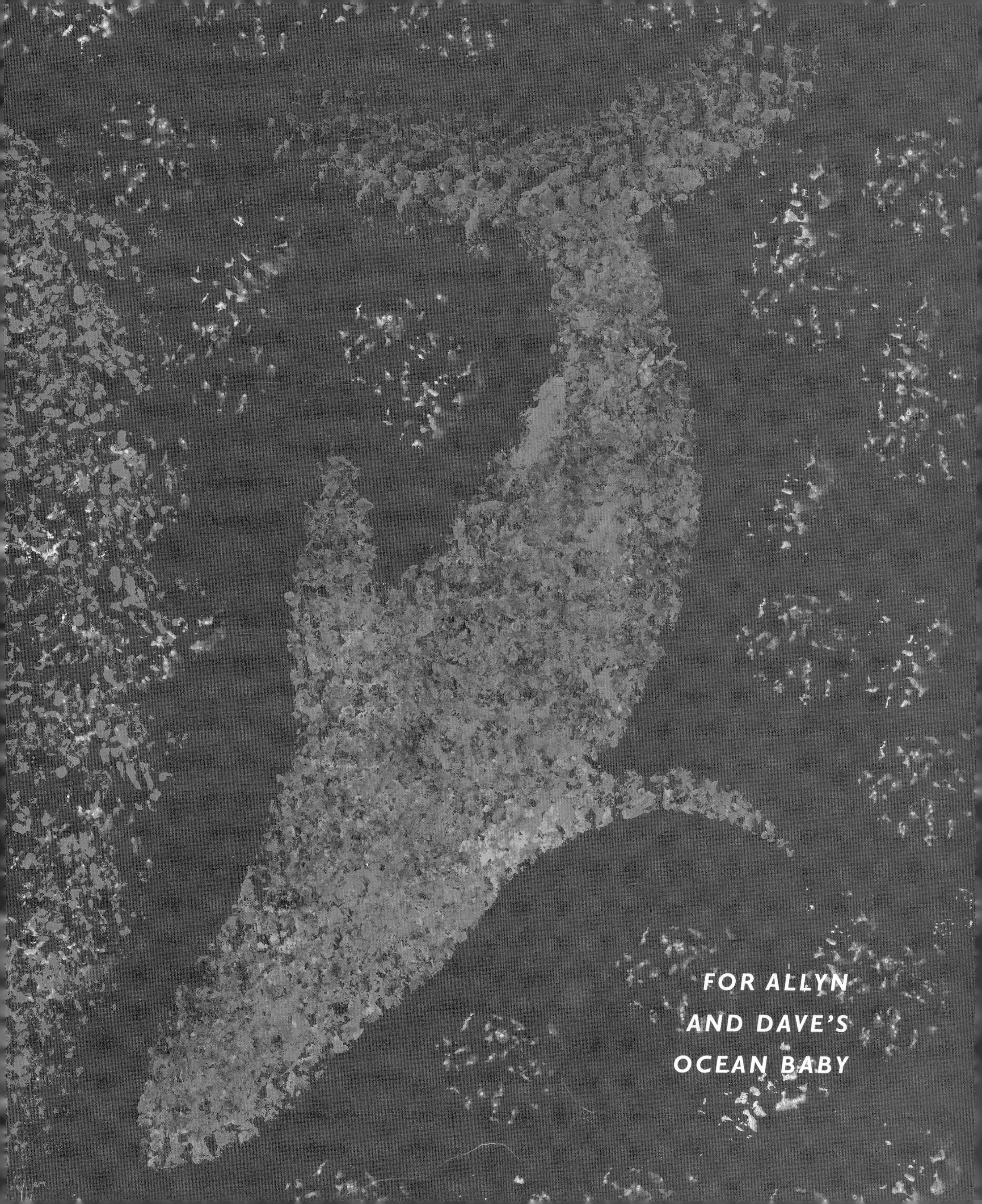

FOR ALLYN
AND DAVE'S
OCEAN BABY

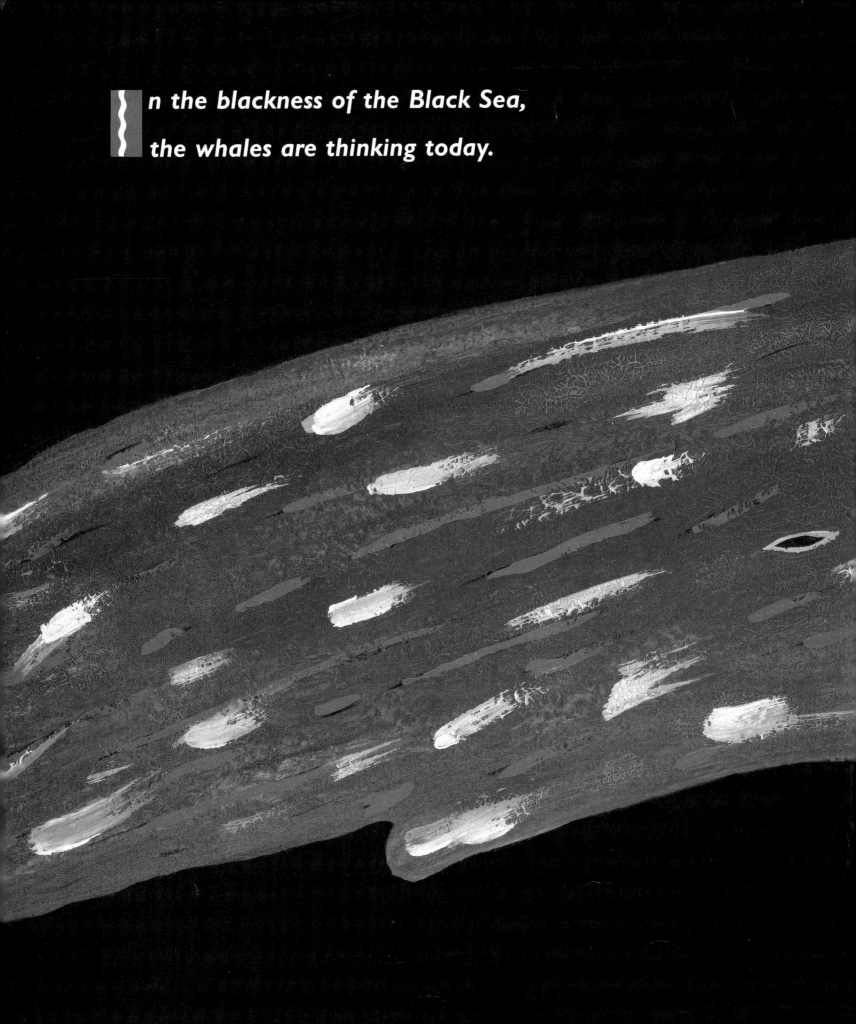

In the blackness of the Black Sea,
the whales are thinking today.

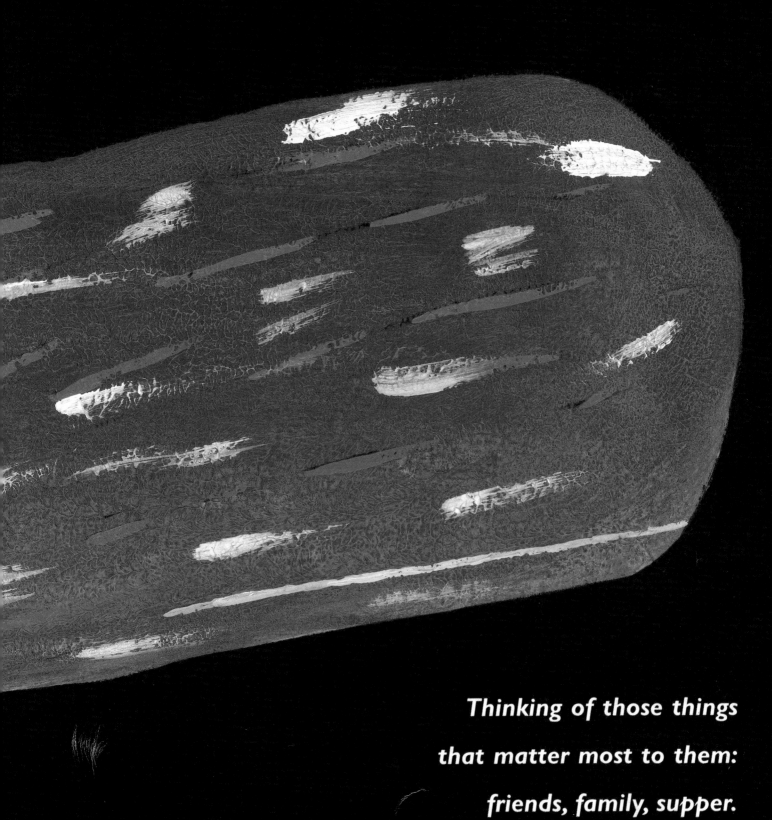

Thinking of those things

that matter most to them:

friends, family, supper.

A song they used to know.

The whales

are thinking

about where

they are going

and how deep

are the oceans

of the world.

They swim in places with beautiful names.

Past Cape Farewell, they say good-bye.

At the Cape of Good Hope, they make a wish.

And under

the Red Sea,

their dreams

are in color.

Whales love their children, and when they are born,
the babies are gently pushed
to the top of the water

where they take their first breath
and see their first sky and gasp
at the loveliness of living.

The Blues are humble.

The largest life God ever made is a blue whale.

Yet blues are neither pushy nor boastful....

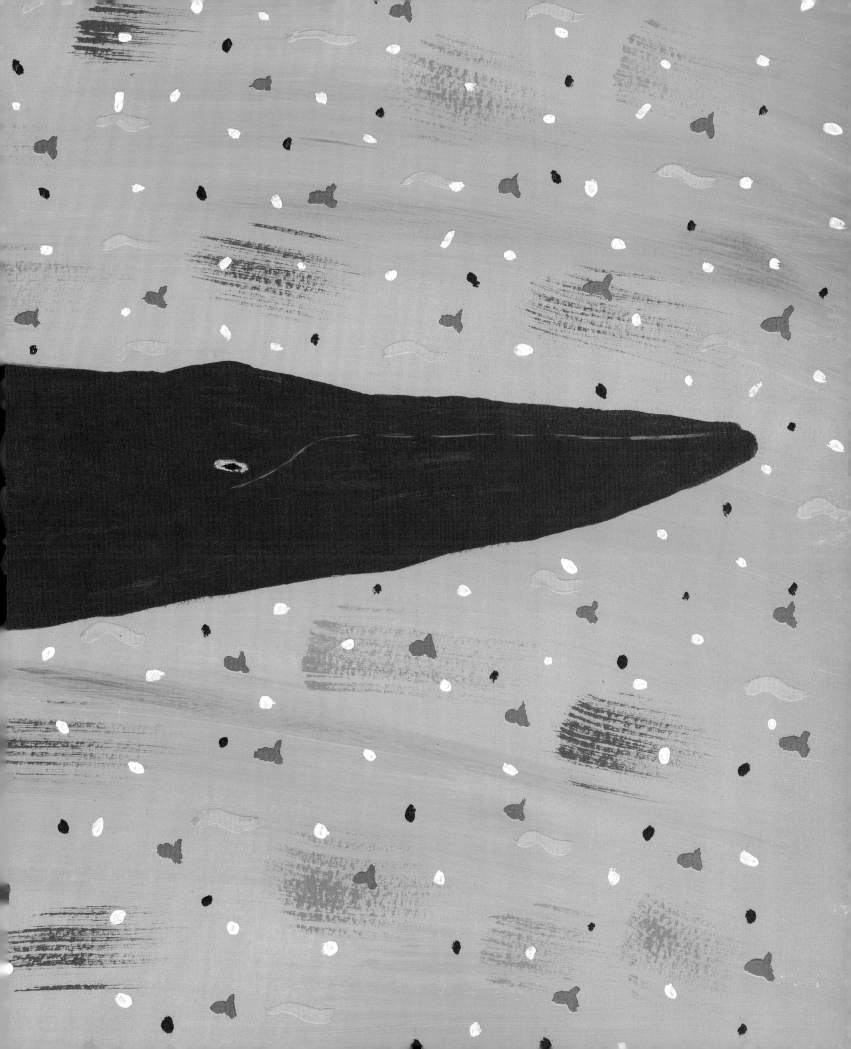

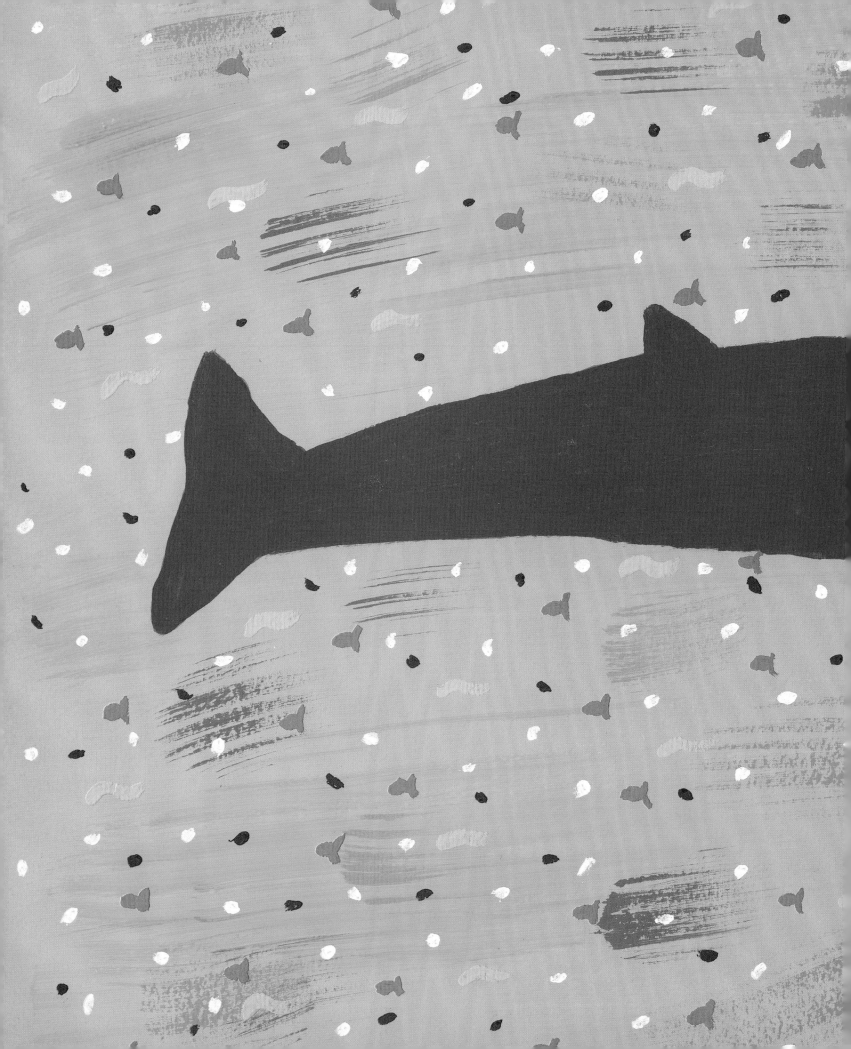

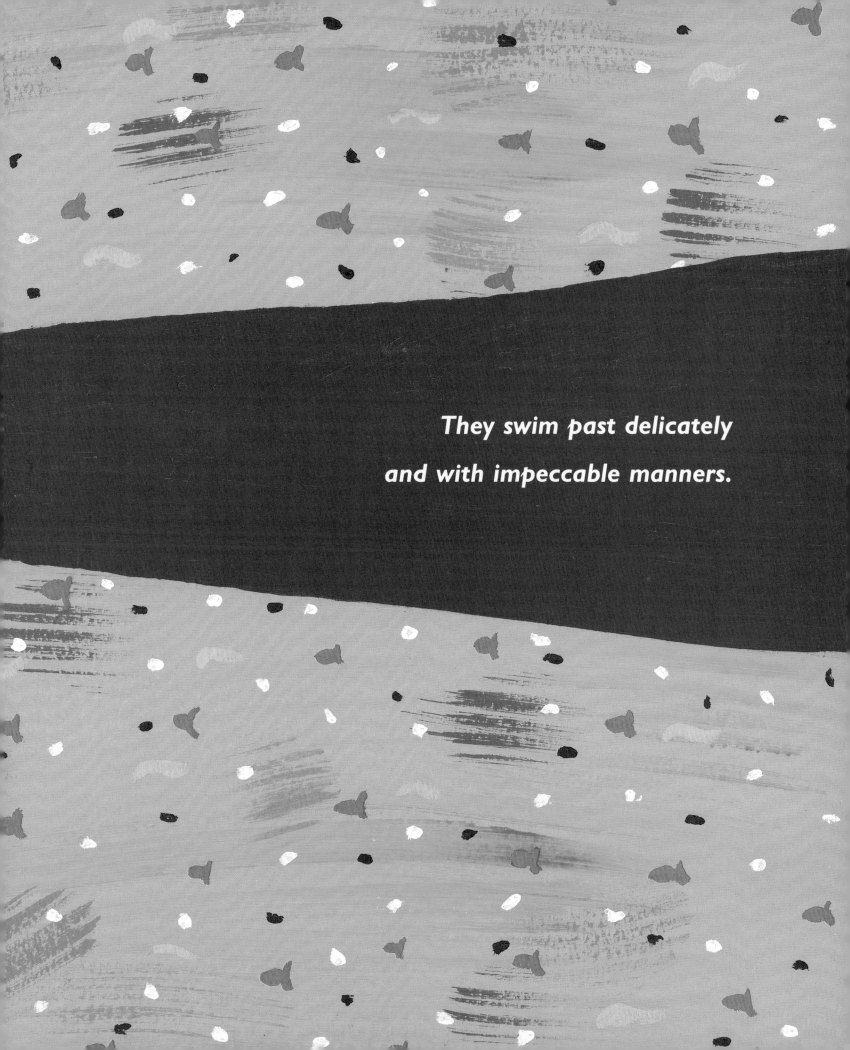

They swim past delicately
and with impeccable manners.

Each Humpback

has a little song to sing,

one all his own,

and as he grows

older and changes,

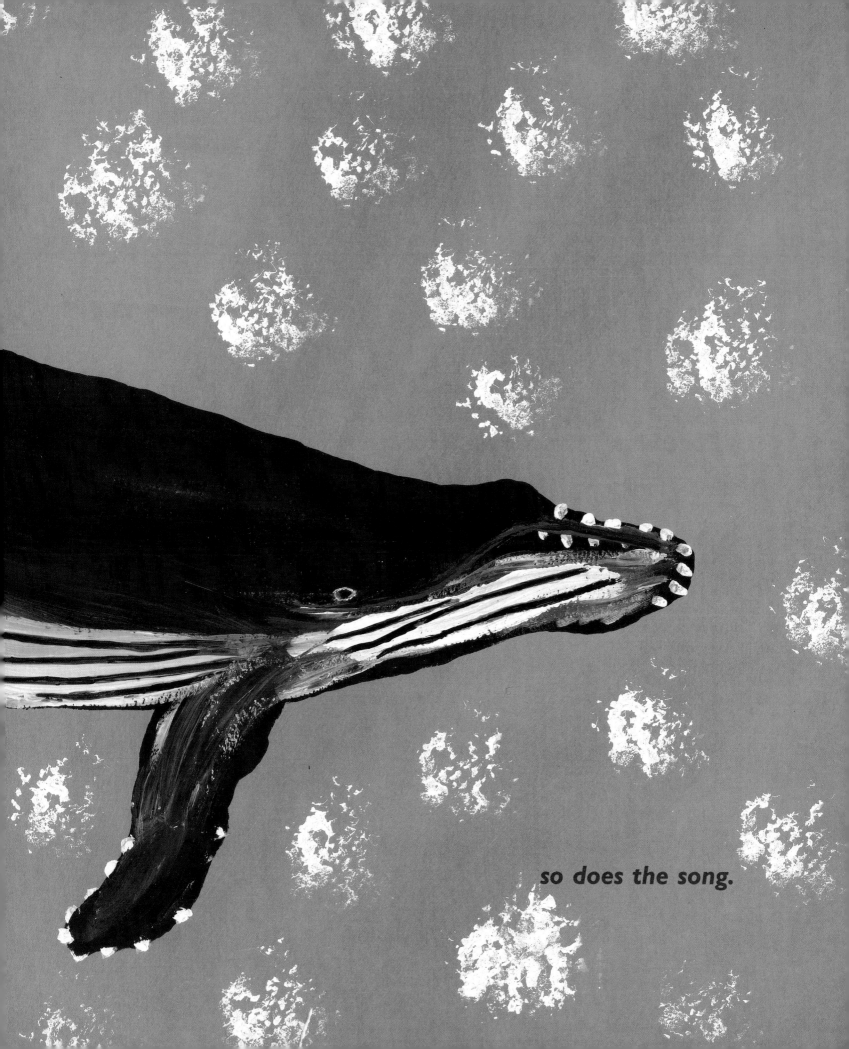

so does the song.

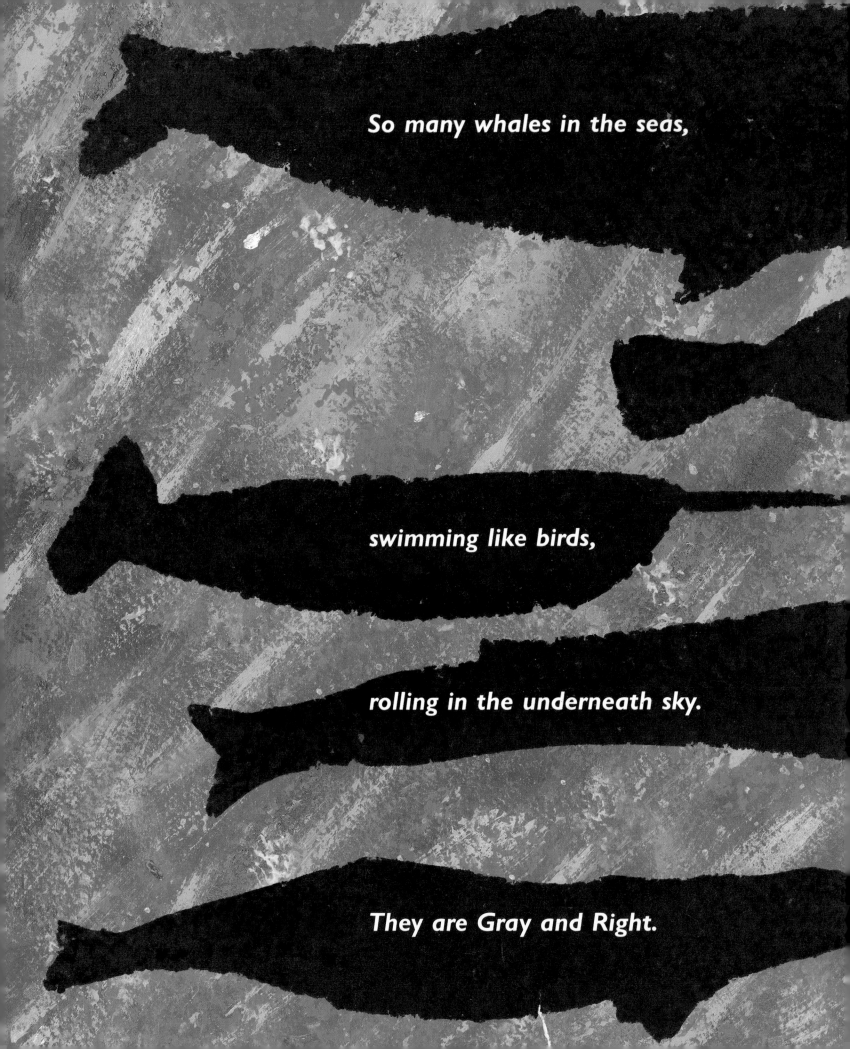

So many whales in the seas,

swimming like birds,

rolling in the underneath sky.

They are Gray and Right.

Beluga and Sperm.

Narwhal and Fin.

They hear everything
and carry secrets between them.

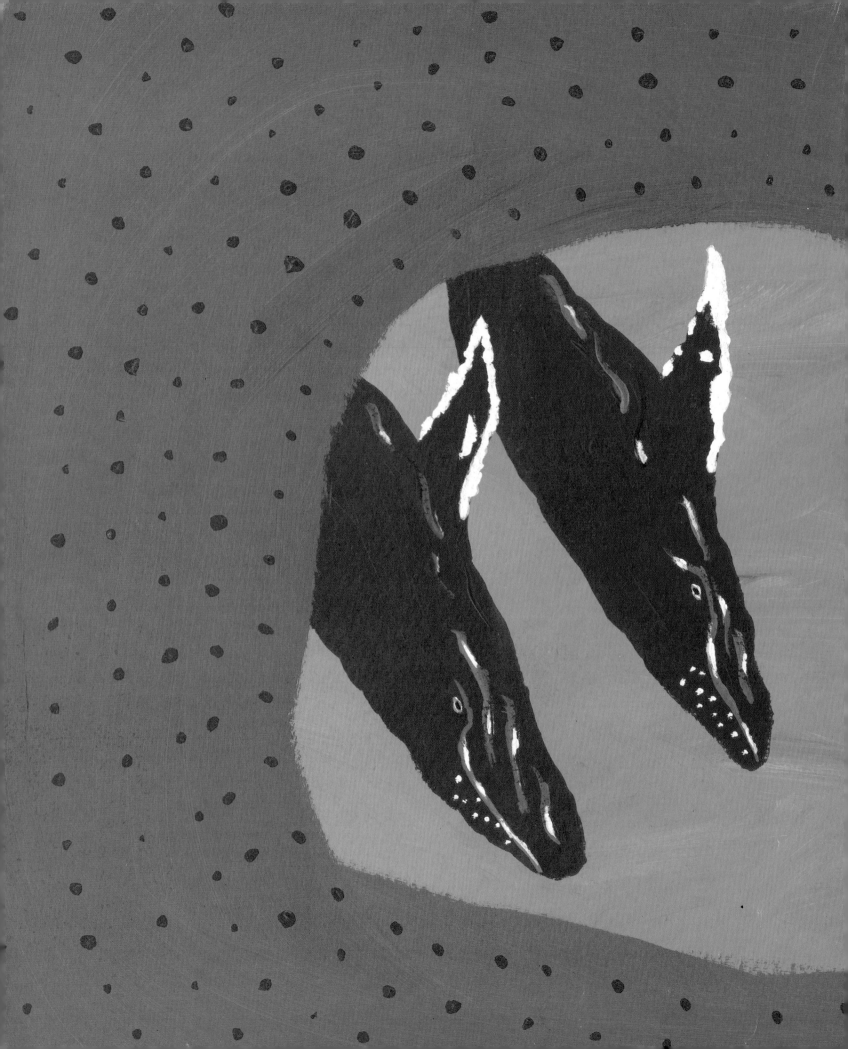

But a rose
is lost on them,
for they haven't
any sense of smell.
No matter.
They love songs
and touching
and can court
without flowers.

O, what they have seen,

swimming from one pole to the other.

What they have seen.

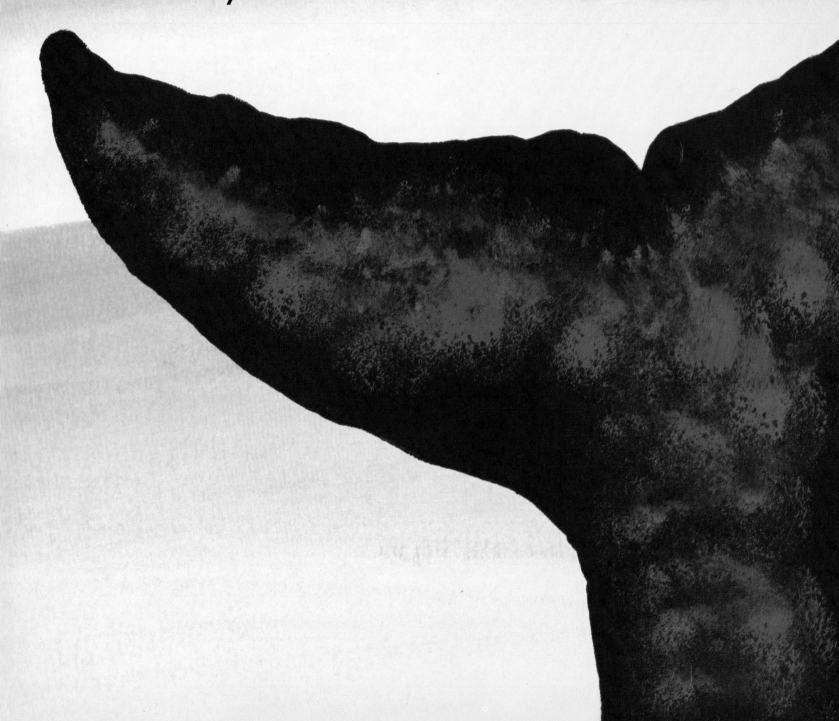

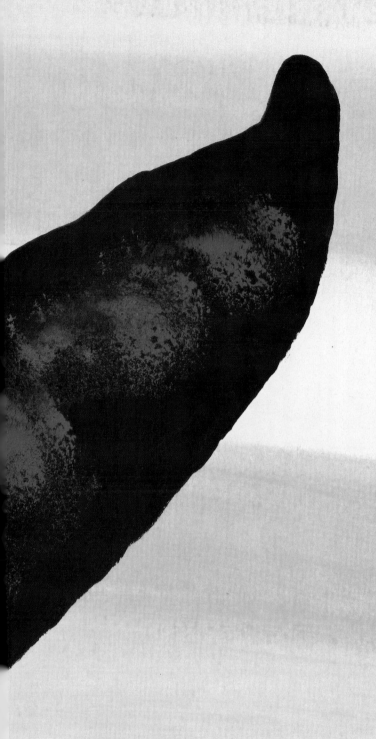

There are not enough poems

in the world to tell. . . .

And whales do not know,

as they rise up for a big breath of air,

that someone is standing on a shore

and his heart is filling up.

Filling up and ready to burst.

Whales do not know how they change people,

how they make them better,

how they make them kind.

Like angels appearing in the sky,

whales are proof of God.

They are swimming today,

in the Indian Ocean,

in the Sea of Japan.

The babies are drinking

their mothers' milk and

their fathers are singing nearby.

They are floating like feathers

in the deep blue green.

They are floating

like feathers

in a sky.

THE WHALES

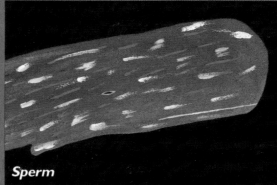
Sperm

Sperm

Right   Humpback

Right

Orca

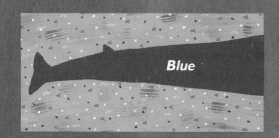
Blue   Blue

Humpback

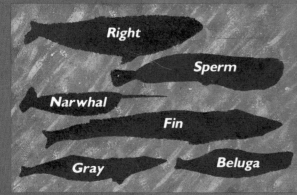
Right
Sperm
Narwhal
Fin
Gray   Beluga

Humpback

Humpback

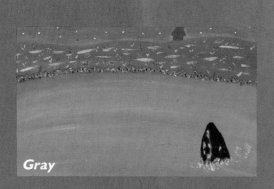
Gray

Humpback

Pilot